A DANCING INNOCENCE

THE DANCER

A DANCING INNOCENCE

TESSA RANSFORD

LINES REVIEW EDITIONS

MACDONALD PUBLISHERS
EDINBURGH

8 2 1

ISBN 0 86334 063 6

Published in 1988 by
Macdonald Publishers
Loanhead, Midlothian EH20 9SY

00549 4468

*The publisher acknowledges
subsidy from the Scottish Arts Council
towards the publication of this volume*

Printed in Scotland by
Macdonald Printers (Edinburgh) Limited
Edgefield Road, Loanhead, Midlothian EH20 9SY

For

ANN D. GWILT

Acknowledgements

Acknowledgements are due to the editors and publishers of the following magazines in which some of the poems in this volume have previously appeared: *Aynd*, *Cencrastus*, *Chapman*, *Lines Review*, *The Fiddlehead* (Canada).

The frontispiece portrays Henri Gaudier-Brzeska's bronze sculpture *The Dancer* (1913) and is reproduced by kind permission of the Tate Gallery, London.

Contents

III—TURN YOURSELF ABOUT

I

ONE-STEP

A DANCING INNOCENCE

"You'll change your life!" wrote Rilke: touched by art—
an archaic torso of Apollo
primed with potent, ancient innocence
to span tomorrow's manic dancing day
on stringent, dark, hyperborean wings
of revolution's prehistoric cause.

Devoid of purpose, casual of cause,
our consciousness may sound the well of art,
empty of feeling empty, night and day
anonymous; but reasonable Apollo
was foiled by Daphne's rooted innocence
and peace descends with tried, dynastic wings.

Ourselves the victims, as we dream of wings
and think our chrysalis an innocence,
with hope shrugged off in having lost a cause.
We suffer whims, abjectly, of Apollo
when ours it is to broach the rising day
with writhing, raw identity of art.

But nothing can be trusted that is art:
the marble is not hewn by fair Apollo.
We do not programme for the brush of wings,
nor tip the edge of consciousness, and cause
unloading of intended innocence
drop by drop to fill each day by day.

The dawning forehead of that destined day
will tear the membranes of our innocence
in brutish births to make a work of art—
and veiled velleities assuming wings,
imaginary Panpipes, will be cause
for mirth before the torso of Apollo.

11

Archaic and yet avant-garde Apollo—
stone to flesh by an essential art;
breath transpires with earth and dream with day,
consubstantiations giving cause
to *Nike* with her huge exultant wings—
and revolution sprung from innocence.

Turn, Apollo. Burn. Outspread and cause
world wings to dare a dancing innocence,
initiation day of perfect art.

BACK TO EARTH

Rilke admired in women Love
that loves without return,
becoming strong, wilder,
overtaking the human object and
finding path to God.

He cited a Portuguese nun
whose letters he translated,
and Gaspara Stampa
who composed two hundred sonnets.

He lists other women
throughout the centuries
who have written and told how they lived
their love
and fed generations with light
from that inexhaustible fuel.

To love, he believed,
achieves in us a reckless security.
The lover, for instance, swims the river,
while the loved one merely waits,
passive, almost a victim.

Love of the godhood in man or of the manhood in God
requires the same flame.
Women have made space in the womb of their minds
for gestating a passion,
giving it birth and rearing it to maturity.

The whole of nature joins in their lament
or their lament is an echo of Earth's lament,
the Goddess herself seeking true husbandmen
in the human.

The question now is not
whether women can still endure,
however dark the world,

or whether they will permit themselves
any more
these foolish obsessions,
or will even prefer to love
and let go
over and over
so that their love may be strong
and unquenchable, like Sappho's,
which thrived on partings
and left her undivided.

The question now is rather
how long Earth can endure
and whether we humans,
attended and loved so long,
can turn, return to her yearning
in time to accept forgiveness
and ask perhaps to be counted
among her servants.

ANNUNCIATIONS

Like butterflies round a lamp
women fluttered to Rilke.
Yet he craved a light in them
with its source in daily things:
in husbands, children, kitchens.

These women, who made their homes,
bread, bouquets, love,
journeys, money,
with earth-sense and practical
attention to particulars,

they were angel-Gabriels
sent to him from the world
to announce to his virgin soul
the conception of poems.

THE POET'S DAUGHTERS

The poet has brought her daughters
to the Commonwealth Literature Conference
and they have brought their knitting.

The knitting is pink and large:
soft balls of wool skewered by needles
lodge casually on a velvet chair
behind the dignitaries.

Bright as Jane Austen's heroines
these young girls miss nothing
behind their chattering needles:

speeches, introductions,
the huffs behind the puff,
poets whose standing
is not on their dignity,
whose words are their own fulfilment.

Eminent names here
could be shattered one day
by a slight chance recollection
of one of these girls, reminiscent,
looking up as she does
from her knitting.

The guillotine rises, falls.

HIGH FLYING

(Cordoba and Granada)

At Cordoba in Spring
I climbed the minaret
twisted dark corners
to reach bright ledges
until in the air I rested;
looked down on the city
river, bridge, country,
tiled roofs, where doves
nestled among the carvings
that cover glades of pillars;
and I beheld the fountain
in the court of orange trees.

Then I lifted my head
and, strangely large,
flew swallows
at eye level.

From towers of the Alhambra
Washington Irving records
men fished for stars
at dusk on summer evenings.
(To catch a living star must be a fearful thing,
to lure a star—with what bait—
but our own eyes gazing?)

But it was not stars they trapped
on those nineteenth-century nights:
they baited hooks with flies
to divert swerving swallows
into knives, nets,
clusters of dead feathers.

EDUCATION AND ENLIGHTENMENT

The teacher assesses the intellect
of every child,
and allocates for it a section of knowledge
as it is divided for convenience
into separate fields,
where those who enter
by degrees may settle quietly
in a neat but narrow corner
and call it a career.

Pedigrees:
no hybrid culture can be countenanced.
Physics may only come with Chemistry,
Greek with Latin, French with German.

What freak mind is this
which wants to resurrect
the energies of dissected knowledge,
holding the parts together
and like a tiger pouncing
from truth to truth?

"Where are the snows of yesteryear?"
In the philosophies of Greece
or in the tragedies?
In minerals of the earth
or the colours of Cezanne?
On the surface of the planets
or in the space within the heart?

Not this and yet not that:
in the tears that flow
from the melted snows of intellect
as each new endeavour
dazzles on a frozen pinnacle
before it cataracts to fertilize
another generation.

MY GRANDDAUGHTER

(at three months)

I embrace in you
the child I am
in your wordless thinking
your serious, sudden focusing
and straightaway delight
at new sensations.

I dandle you on my knee
and it is myself.
I have been dreaming of babies:
they rejuvenate within me,
having completely nought.

In my older age I seem to
assume years remain
and plan how best to accommodate
the lack, the losses . . .

but parts of me keep starting life
again today and again,
learn to express themselves,
crawl, walk, babble, bite what is new
and make things work
together in my mind
for good, and people
for love . . .
love.

I AND THOU

*Open Day at the Queen's Stables,
Redford Barracks, May 1977*

Lodged high on the stable bars
one man
was talking to his horse,
the long-boned head between his hands
in timeless conversation.

Beneath him people walked and stared,
men groomed and cleaned and fed
their horses, took them to be shod
or polished kit and tack.

Great-black-high-standing-horse,
other, apart,
yet massively yourself;
thoroughly you know this man,
not his rank, his name, his education,
nothing of what pertains to him,

but you know him:
his voice, his touch, his genius,
as he and you commune
in gentle, total, holiness.

PRAYER FOR MY CHILDREN

I pray for you my children.
I tell you, my beads, over and over,
but my prayers are not to God
or any such alien power,
nor do I pray out of fear
for your safety or happiness.

Like a chant I utter the names
allotted your new-born existence
filled out by your own meaning,
fleshed with your personality.

I sing your names with pride,
for each of you is worth
a hundred possible poems.

Like stars, like flowers or footsteps
running towards me, your bodies
shine, your imaginations describe
a unique calligraphy.

I repeat your names and conjure your graces.
I award you medals for loving and
citations for courage.

I used to be able to help
or comfort or lead the way,
but now I see you have
overtaken me and become
skilful in ways I shall never know.

Words alone are my daily gift,
the bread I feed you.
Like a cow licking its calf
I recite your names
in strong warm rhythms.

THIS

Inspired by the Russian film Farewell

This is the tree that will not fall;
This the soil that holds our dead;
Here a house grew into home.

Flowers are here that do not fail,
A field, and pathway to the shore.
That music is the voice of birds
And slow mourning of the herds.

These our children with their eyes
Watching, and their questions;
The cat has somewhere disappeared
As we shall do beneath the waves
To slake the fire we set alight
Ourselves to consecrate the past.

And I shall consecrate the past
Illumined in my memory;
I shall drown in the length of years
All passions of the moment;
Eyes of mine shall stare again
Like children, but at no thing.

Dogs and cat, birds and cattle
Move in my habitual ways;
My field is green and blows with flowers
Which do not fail within their season;
My home I build, it grows in me.
In deep earth I store my dead
Who live like rings upon my tree.
This tree, this life that will not fall.

GIRL RAKING HAY: 1918

She laughs in the hayfield, sixteen, slight,
over her shoulder a chestnut plait,
broad-brimmed hat
and long skirt,
summer, hay day, August heat,
1918, peace not yet.

The huge hayrake is twice her size,
the hands that wield it, like lilies;
death the news,
her brother dies.
While girls all yearn for armistice
the hay falls scythed about their knees.

TO MY MOTHER,
OLD AND FORGETFUL

It's time to leave and I hug you,
all that is you in my life
as I let it go.

I leave the world as new,
when snowdrops were new and puppies
and travel and books
and my own body was new,
my clothes and shoes
because I was growing.

I leave my sense of home:
your tweeds and brooches,
the paintings you did of trees,
your old desk and three-cornered chair,
the green and white vase for flowers
from the garden you made wherever you lived;

your voice that speaks my name,
your hands, the way they loved
my children and showed it
in deeds over and over.

Before my memory worked
I lived in you, in your mind.
Now I do the remembering
and tell you who you were and
where you are
and what we are doing now,

as I leave you receding
into the future.
It will coil and join up
with the past
and we'll be together
as always.

CENTREPIECE

The yacht in the midst of the bay
is ringed with eyes.
It sways in its own conceit
in a swirl of seas
far from the lesser fleet
moored alongside the quai.

The yacht in the midst of the bay
dances and turns
dips its flag and mast
bows and leans
towards each observant host
with appropriate ceremony.

The yacht in the midst of the bay
is a point of light
in a garland, a festival
of illumined night:
single, vulnerable,
mañana it sails away.

ELEGY

Willows are growing in the lake
and larches in the shallows;
tiny stars flower in the water
and white birds float upon it;
grass and bracken shape the paths
where drovers grazed their cattle;
a tribe is buried beneath the mound
family by ancient family;
a Mabinogian hound splashes
in and out of the mere.

I stumble with my conflicting sorrows:
grief that my mother is dying
and acceptance that she would wish it.
Her courage and high adventure—
may these carry her over the lake
like shadow of cloud across it.
The wind is murmuring in the larches
and wings of sailing birds.

Among the willows my grief is growing:
this earth is shedding her slowly.
The world around shall be empty of her
but my world only more full.

TEA DANCE

A May afternoon in the Assembly Rooms, George Street
a tea-dance, thé-dansant, strict tempo band.

With memories of dancing all night in the fifties
ballroom and Scottish, beneath the chandeliers,
kilts and shining dresses, pumps and dainty slippers,
I found a crowd gathered of elderly ladies
seated at tables before each mirrored mural
as if for coffee-morning or the girl-guide jumble.

The band set the pace with foxtrot, quickstep
quick quick slow, like life itself
and finally the tango, no subservience here.
Scorning cups of tea, grey-haired they rose,
danced with each other, dancing as they could,
two or three men shared around between them.
Youth and beauty do not count when there's music,
when feet know what to do, heads know how to turn.
Chandeliers glittered, old tunes glinted,
and the ladies, neat-ankled, turned, stepped
out, rocked, progressed and twirled like girls
in some complicated playground memory game.

Buried are their partners, their days with pleasure in them,
lang syne their beaux.
But they kept their gold sandals
and the patterns, and the rhythm of dancing in their bones.

THE DHOBI'S DOG

Dhobi ka kutta na ghar ka na ghat ka
(the washerman's dog belongs neither to house nor riverside)

The dhobi's dog will return from riverbank in the sun
to the house, but not lie down, to and fro he'll trot,
panting, semi-wild, hither and thither recalled,
never petted, fondled, either hot or cold.
Does he belong? to whom? Dhobi-ji sends him home,
Bibi-ji won't give him room. Such is my lot.

Born and reared in India: comforted by ayah,
on some cool verandah of lofty bungalow,
with charpai and degchi, decanter and serahi;
enervated, dusty, the whining mosquito,
black ants and red, huge fans overhead:
when all was done and said, the British had to go.

In Scotland I froze: hands, feet, nose,
in thick uneasy clothes at dour boarding school:
a wind-resistant, dismal, stern, redoubtable,
grey-stone-wall life exemplified by rule,
embarrassed to embrace, weep, laugh, kiss:
was I of this race? from such a gene pool?

I lived in Pakistan, land of the Mussulman,
governed by the Koran. I learnt Punjabi,
dressed in shalwar, travelled to Lahore,
joined in zabur, lived on dal-chapati:
but didn't my passport say "British, born Bombay"
however long my stay in Sialkot or Karachi?

I like the way I speak, the voice my thoughts make,
yet Scottish folk are quick to call me English.
I've lived here twenty years (Anderson forebears
and Glasgow Macalisters—that's baksheesh!)
Still my language finds no place, no ethnic dress or face:
I plead my special case and thus I finish.

REQUIREMENTS (Lewis)

These ancient stones
    for their hallowing—
ancient of earth
    before their upsetting
as markers and
    measurers of the skies—
require no pathway
    or hardened track
no authority
    garbed in black
no electric light
    closed doors
sonorous prayers
    squared walls.

Nor do they require
    cans of beer
cigarettes
    conspiracy
transistor sets
    micro-gear
beside the wind-white beaches.

Rocks are banded
    rose and clear
        like warm skin
waves are lucent
    grey-green
        of reflective eyes
a sudden sunrise
    breaks into rooms
        of makeshift houses
a reel of flowers
    dances around
        rusting cars
spray resounds
    in the gully near
        the cemetery.

29

WATER, WEST COAST

It seems as though the principal element
from which all things derive in the west is waves,
   is water, water, water, only
      water, the ultimate end of substance.

The quartzite vein that runs through the mountain rock
becomes a cataract in a night of rain;
   the road a river; rocks and trees are
      manifestations of water's essence.

And sunshine seeps, distils from a molten core,
displays through rainbow seaward in slanting rays;
   the moon is ice, is crystal, hardened,
      blanching the ocean and dwindling shoreline.

Our very breathing knows itself born of mist;
our limbs and fingers flow into coiling streams
   whose current courses through the body,
      thickens to densities when we waver.

The boats, the houses, shops, and the wooden pier;
the heron, oyster-catcher and dipping swan;
   the curlew's cry a floating ripple;
      water, the soul of the land and people.

AUTUMN IN APPIN

To lie awake in the sound of the stream and praise the gods
of the place: the clear god of the river whose chant ceaselessly
flows; whose course is strong, perpetual, like the heart
when it floods and knows in love no beginning, no ending;
numberless green gods who stir in oak and alder
or form tender mosses, clothing the oldest walls;
the god of the disused mill, his huge quernstone idle—
to acknowledge these, and a host of enduring divinities,
is to be slowly enlivened in unused cells of the brain
and tuned, every sense in harmony with the others;
aware, without meditation or strenuous exercise
of the will, or body positions; to expand into the human,
allow ourselves to become what we know already we are.

Birds—messengers—pass from world to world,
make themselves visible and summon us with their music;
rowanberries shine in their own luminosity
blood-red in leaves decaying into gold;
brambles taste of darkness, ripen in the rain;
a castle on its toy island stands erect,
sign of sombre history in the wilderness.

An owl left a feather hanging in a branch
for me to gather and keep as token of this day.

NOCTURNE (Lewis)

It is raining on Lewis in the night;
Darkness has brimmed over the hills
spilling upon the moor
and dropping into circles of inland sea.

Last night the moon was wildly shed
by mountain and cloud to reveal a sheer
countenance at the window
and blending with the water in bright festoons;

but tonight the dark is raining on Lewis:
on the black-house with its hunched thatch
on battered, abandoned buses,
derelict cars and stacks of murky peat.

Boats are plying under the rain
and enormous eels under the boats
and fishing nets are lifted
up and under the tide like diving birds.

For thousands of years of nights the stones
have loomed in lonely communion
beneath the moon, the rain,
ritually aloof, cleansed and illumined.

And the white schist of my lasting self
safe and awake yet exposed to love—
its darkness and shafts of light—
takes up position in line with primeval wisdom.

II

TWO-STEP

MAKING SENSE

A POEM SEQUENCE ON THE FIVE SENSES, SET IN PARIS

The poems refer to the medieval tapestry of *La Dame à la Licorne*, which is thought to be an allegory of the five senses, at the Musée de Cluny in Paris. There is a sixth tapestry with above and below on it the words A MON SEUL DESIR and LE CHOISIR DES BIJOUX.

AUBADE:
On the author's crossing into France

LE CHOISIR DES BIJOUX

What crossing now through life I make
It is for my beloved's sake.

What reason takes me from his side,
Both Time and Place shall be defied.

What fame I find, new interest,
Nothing can my love contest.

What country, people, culture, art
I choose . . . with him I keep my heart.

This sea I sail to enter France
Serves but to strengthen our alliance.

Our love grows closer despite this absence
And finds its own peculiar presence.

I'll end within his circling arm
From wandering through hurt and harm.

The flow of love in all sustains,
Calls forth the message it contains.

I have in love the world—and more—
Wisdom, song, poetic lore.

I bring my Love, as to the world,
The choice of treasures I have culled.

I. LA VUE (*Sight*)

The seer dreads his second-sight
from which there's no awakening as from dream,
rather no further sleep.

To observe without ego
and peer between bulbous, gargoyle selves:

to realign distortion,
shatter light, filter space:

to spy, with interior cosmic eye,
cerulean and jade of water-colour
earth ochre, umber,
flecks of fire,
filigree of silver and firmaments of gold:

these captured by the eye,
daub the varied facets of the soul
which glint as if with mica and subterranean minerals.

To visualise crystals:

the eye of *l'esprit* selects *dans la nuit*
without advisers,
loneliest observer of infinities:

"Le choisir des bijoux"

*   *   *

Eve with her serpent is locked in coils of prophecy
as Rodin set her, inextricably, in marble
with her natal, fatal thirst for unity
such as contemplation could not satisfy alone
that moist, writhing grapple for enlightenment,
never handed over on a plate.

Dimly in the forest without contamination
we regard in a mirror Medusa or La Licorne
nor stare them in the face, like imbeciles,
the creatures of our pure imagination.

The eye shall not rest on hardening surfaces
of uncongealed gestalt,
but speculate beyond the boundary
toward memory and liberty.

II. L'OUIE (*Hearing*)

Far from telephone and traffic, ambulance and siren,
a young man stamps and shouts in his addiction
during abbreviated hours of summer dark
when silence breaks his nerve:

while in mountains by the choral river
a single stag barks at dusk,
a lark is not in vain.

To be heard we must utter out of silence
but we find none.

Drums have come to Paris and permeate our pleasures,
repeated exclamations without punctuation
marking nothing, beating air:
popular decrees: of the people, to the public, for the populace.

Equanimity is not made in unison.

Music, lingua franca of the sundry soul,
is hardly heard above the shriek of children
and rampage of vehicles.

The same voice issues from every french window—
vulgar commentator on the common life.

Let us lay our ear to the breast of the beloved
and listen to vibrations in the body
when we breathe each other's names:

then break into silence after whisperings of love,
and after song of ecstasy, a requiem.

III.   L'ODORAT (*Smell*)

If I savour wine among the poets of Paris
shall I know the bouquet of those
who will prove good?

"My genius is in my nostrils"
wrote Nietzsche, scenting SuperMensch
with divine maliciousness.

Bridges badly built will come tumbling down;
a well-made poem may become a parapet
or vine-duct of the vintage year,
each verse-ful worthy of libation.

The cult of self-expression puffs incense
among its heady worshippers
as they snuffle after "genuine experience."

An aesthetic aroma is not achieved by accident:
the herbs are planted, cultured,
cooked precisely with every virtue balanced,
passed from one to another in some upper room
where the initiated enter
who have followed the sign:

A man with a pitcher? A woman with poems?

The perfume is like summer earth at evening after rain.

IV. LE GOUT (*Taste*)

Homo Sapiens: Mankind only wise:
she who sips, he who sups,
sapper, tapper:

we who draw the sap and dip the sop
who live sapiently
by testing, tasting, teasing out,
trying on the tongue
the flavours of experience,
sucking every succulence.

How else to know the new,
find future fuel?
Temptation is essential:
how else essay the essences
savour *le savoir*?

Goblin Market, whose syrup poisons purity,
Eve's evil:
serpent-toothed virtuosity—bitter—
better left unbitten?

In risking reproduction we may lose more than a rib.

To sample each spirit and stir again
a cocktail of creation:
intoxication
but rising to the surface
realisation.

This and this is to my taste,
suits my saliva,
comme il faut,
demanded by my pool of DNA
to flood for my salvation,
enhance my special quality of soul.

Milk and honey for the masses:
taste ye all of this;
bread and fishes for the multitude,
no soul-sated fatness:
body, yes, and blood,
waxing and waning of the substances.

A dose of freedom is vinegar to thirst;
a mouthful of independence is sprinkled with salt.
Then no reversion to slavery,
no guzzling at the breast.

Spew the lukewarm,
dare a daily wilderness,
for grapes are gigantic in the land of promise.

V.   LE TOUCHER (*Touch*)

Noli me tangere:
do not touch the man-made-god
who must remain intact.

Do not touch leper, sweeper, outcast, untouchables,
contamination!

Intangible taboos
whose texture is of tapestry:
when close-up the pattern is untraceable.

Golden is the Mean
worked out by measurement, '
the span, cubit, pace:
balanced and peized methodically by science,
trial and error,
achieving the right touch,
getting the true feel of it:
tact.

Do not touch exhibits made by human hand—
FRAGILE—
dust has a property to return to dust
and there is no insurance against that assurance.
Let the *objets* gather dust, never dirty fingermarks.

Not so the tea-bowl, cupped in both hands
ceremonially passed
lips to its lip,
whose slight imperfections are lovingly fingered,
signs of authority.

Every man an artist
who takes life in his hands
tentatively models his own soul,

42

tangent on each other's
circles, cubes, spires, aspirations,
interior labyrinth
with double-headed axe
severing the substance, except the finest thread.

Keep us in touch:
let us build cathedrals with tactful, arching fingers,
touch—each other on the raw,
move to tears,
wake each other every dawn with kisses.

VI. THE SIXTH SENSE (*Intuition*)

SICUT UMBRA DIES NOSTRI
—*sundial in court of La Sorbonne*

Lacy ironwork
slitted shutters
spidery facades
Paris balconies
antennae onto regimented streets
for regulated moods of quiet vivacity.

"La vie de Paris
ç'a n'est pas Paradis"
goes le chanson à Montmartre.

Do not mention the children to Marie Antoinette
for their shadows never lengthened
and she went into darkness from her life with the Sun.

It was for the cause of *liberté*
"Lebensraum"
which the Nazi general spared from orders of destruction
and his shadow was shot short.

Napoleon is hero
and only sparrows, shadowless, sport upon the grass,
little fluffs of freedom to whom nought is interdit.

It was to win *egalité*:
nick-nacks and knickers in la rue de Rivoli,
kisses on both cheeks,
cavalry at Concorde on le quatorze juillet.

It aimed at *fraternité*:
parade of people through pipelines of culture,
moved by escalator
in the Pompidou Centre where artists rub shoulders,
the flamboyant and the functional:
structuralism, feminism,
the French a sex apart.

44

Beyond the wrought-iron door lies a scrubbed yard.
The fat concierge will unlock no secrets
but climb l'escalier,
quietly red-carpeted,
to greetings with champagne
and the petit, private balcony:

A birthday celebration?
The future contracts as our shadow stretches
and art by its rays makes our days but passing shades.

"Vraiment Madame! Vous êtes une grande âme."

ENVOI:

On the author's returning to Britain.

A MON SEUL DESIR

Travelling now to Calais the white road
I return with poems in my load.

To little, *grande* isle with whose tongue
I lick my poems into shape and song.

Farewell *le paysage, les boulevards*,
City effusive, courteously on guard,

In gallery or peddled on the street
Aesthetically relentlessly élite.

The elemental senses here refined
Are fashioned within studios of the mind.

Decorated with austere caress
Formulated with soft seriousness.

As now I turn from stately avenue
Poems, *mes feuilles, ce sont mes bijoux.*

*Comme la Dame au milieu de mille fleurs
J'envoie mes poèmes à mon seul desir.*

WOUNDING OF THE BRIGHT

*"With grandiose resolve a man endeavours to soar above all
obstacles, but this encounters a hostile fate."*
—from the *I-Ching*

I read in you the book of changes,
friend, poet, superior man,
who soared high above all obstacles.

First I read the majuscule
now gaunt, pale, delicate,
illuminated white with beard and hair,

flowing like the salmon river
where your back was broken
where you never ceased to wade deeper.

Eyes, letters, lips, are pale
when brightness has been wounded
and wings of courage forced to waive and fold.

You could not rise or turn your head,
you could not eat or drink
nor digest the thoughts encased in books.

Convalescent, you sit in darkness,
hands large, weak,
that felt the tugging wind across the loch.

Remaining true to principles
imposed upon yourself,
your voice has now withdrawn within your breast;

and now the obstacles you overcame,
including your own will,
have snatched you down into their old complaints

and you are forced to live on secret food,
to tap an inward source,
through which you are transfigured in our view.

47

THE EGYPTOLOGIST

He lives on the edge of the desert
and shifts the sand
rising at dawn
in winter
when each grain glistens
with cold.

He sifts through an ancient tomb,
minutely records it,
slowly draws
conclusions
about the early
Egyptians.

In Summer his lecture-tours
disclose to the world
what was uncovered—
while silently
sand slips back
into place.

Snatched for a moment from dust,
stolen from desert
after days
of cold digging
a fragment of life
warms up,

and in academic reports
a body of knowledge
is carefully
mummified
for future
generations.

THE CITY WE LIVE IN

You are on my skyline
as high as eye is lifted
nothing is beyond you.

I approach and
come up against
walls
your rock defences.

You bridge my extremes
lead over, across
between one level and another.

I pass within the shadow
of your arches
and walk the colonnade.

Crescent and high terrace
would not entice me but
for sudden vista:

statue, campanile,
pearl of sea, jade of hill
well-proportioned temple.

More than these
I try the narrow steps
tunnelled wynds, wrought-iron gates

that lead me where
an inner court
holds itself secluded.

IN THE ROYAL BOTANIC GARDEN

After the sculptures have been removed to the New Scottish
Gallery of Modern Art in John Watson's School, 1985

"That was Henry Moore's *Reclining Woman*"—
    He pointed out a shape of yellowed grass
    where the large recumbent stone
    had welcomed clamb'ring children,
    tentative caresses.
"And there stood Epstein's *Christ*
    Christian soldier-like
    sentinel of the city
    watchman who never slept."

I looked toward the trees beside the path
where first I saw that figure,
the city spread before him;
and always, looking up,
I'd know a stab of stern respect:
he could have bowed down
to have the kingdoms of this world.

"Once a girl rose from the lily pond—
    a nymph with head inclined,
    as all below her and around
    diverse fishes glinted."

These figures now have been transplanted,
plucked as no gardener would do,
no soil taken with them,
no attentive placement
to placate their genius.

We feel their absent presence
where once we used to meet them,
sense the exile they must know
in having left their Eden,
and the loss we find
in this unpeopled garden.

TRAGEDY

I know the pain of pity and of fear,
my left and right in walking down the street:
I feel, because I love and I admire.

Grieving as I go, I bend and bear
within my heart and head uneasy weight
that tells the pain of pity and of fear.

This balance of emotion, now and here,
not far or future, false or indiscrete,
I risk, because I love and I admire.

One walks the road towards me, passing near,
whom daily I converse with when we meet,
and touch the pain of pity and of fear.

I only sense what fate he must endure
but surely know his excellence complete:
I weep, because I love and I admire.

My own condition is becoming clear:
I cannot save myself nor yet retreat
but take this pain of pity and of fear.

No need to seek the origin of error;
we suffer for the vision we create.
I write, because I love and I admire.

I carry gifts of joy and trust and care
and burnish them in shadow of defeat.
I know the pain of pity and of fear;
I feel, because I love and I admire.

'THE NERVES SIT CEREMONIOUS'

—Emily Dickinson

Now is time for ceremony,
for protocol, hush, removal of shoes,
for contemplation, breathing slowly,
spine strengthened, to distance
the turbulent heart with its woes
and reduce its cravings to silence.

Five or six have overrun
my apartment in trendy outfits.
They rifle my fridge, open my oven.
They gobble, dance, shout,
spill things, turn on music,
everything thrown about.

I meant to invite my chosen friends,
prepare a meal, sample their talk
quietly, so that human sounds
are not disguised, so that weight
transforms to wit and wisecrack,
or gesture of understanding.

But this I must forgo.
I deny myself any intimacy
with intruders, though
civil and douce they appear
at first: no desire, sympathy:
this bereavement is private, pure.

DER ZEIT IHRE KUNST
DER KUNST IHRE FREIHEIT*

That Young Style discovered
time complicated
space limited
people a mosaic
in slinky golden patches.

Women were free to let down their snakes.

Waves breasted against the rim
of nine times nine the cosmos
and showed their intimate structure
as never since Leonardo.

Plants stretched on spindly stems.

Three wise men turned into owls,
tolerant furies.

Salamanders were suspended by a coiling Celtic tail.

The dome of that Age
was grown from golden leaves
whose light glanced from surfaces
and entered into curves
placed according to dimensions of freedom.

I see, not masonry, but eyes
engraved, and light reflected
swooping
like birds from a niche.

The Older Age had fashioned its art out of violence
soothed it with solos from Vienna singing-boys
caged in a gilt chapel
kyrie eleison . . .
to the reassuring rhythm of fiacre ponies, blinkered,
trotting round the Ring, round and round.

To each art its own discovery of freedom.

The walls Wagner could not build
Klimt could not decorate.
Medicine could not rescue Egon Schiele from the 'flu.
The Law could not take away the sufferings of the weak
nor Philosophy obviate the disciplines of freedom.

Klimt painted women saturated with desire
and was dubbed a pornographer.
To show them subdued, raped, genuflecting
is sacred art?
He painted trees and flowers
peasants' homes, barns:
"A building should wear its own kind of clothing
not look like something else
but seem to be itself."

Can women win the freedom to be themselves
like houses?
That art has yet to come of age.

What abode can we build
if we have lost our image?

Scotland was welcome in the heart of Europe when
Charles Rennie Mackintosh
breathed his designs into sparkling Vienna
and himself inhaled
the early-morning breezes
of that sacred spring.

The powers that worshipped power
fought a war to end all wars
and another age was spoiled
of its fragile art,
another art was shackled
for having tasted freedom.

* TO THE AGE ITS ART
  TO THE ART ITS FREEDOM

Inscription over the Secession building in Vienna built by Olbruch about 1900.
It was erased by the Germans but later restored.

EPISTLE

"To dearest Him who lives, alas, away"
                                        —HOPKINS

To "dearest him who lives, alas, away"
I send this letter, not in hope or thought
it may arrive, or that he might reply:
"Dead letter" written as a last resort,
no communication, but report
on life within my person reaching forth
to join the polar self, from south to north.

*   *   *

I write to those dear ones whose lives have spoken
beyond their lives, and even into mine:
Tagore, whose *Gitanjali* was a token
of waiting slow for nascent love to shine
however poor and unprepared my shrine,
growing in consciousness without dismay,
becoming lovely in love's cosmic play.

To John MacMurray for his lucid word:
two people are a person when related;
water of faith has only to be stirred
to free the self from circumstances fated,
from depending on the very fear it hated,
until the world is interdwelt by love
and footsteps walk upon the moving wave.

*   *   *

George Fox, for your experience of the light
of God within us all, for the way
Christ opened hidden things and spoke outright
to your condition, and to mine today;
how silence lets us hear what he would say;
your witness against barriers of words
or wars, throughout this good world of the Lord's.

55

I thank you for the chance of worshipping
daily in life without need of a priest;
for men and women quietly gathering
free of dogma, rigmarole and feast;
for sign and sacrament in every least
concern or prayer, spilling from the centre
where God in us and we in God may enter.

*   *   *

Teilhard de Chardin, to you most of all
I write, because you satisfied my mind
by showing that it is an upward fall
toward spirit and communion of mankind
in sea and earth and universe we find;
all diversities answer their milieu
Christ—within, without, alpha and omega.

Both east and west, in science and religion
throughout your life, in travel and exile,
all opposites were in creative union:
from facts of matter spirit grew fertile
becoming more alive and volatile
until within the consciousness of Man
a new threshold of love and life began.

Not only in the past of evolution
but present in our midst to be revealed
in daily life and every least decision,
all increase and all wastage of the world,
the breathing of the body of the Lord.
To be entirely human and yet humble
leaves room enough to be entirely hopeful.

*   *   *

Solzhenitsyn, often to you I turn
my thoughts: centred you stand, rock of ages,
Paul-archetype: lighthouse to guard and warn
against more spreading death, our world's wages.

Your Gethsemane of written pages,
while we were finding rest and ease on earth,
makes suffering the measure of our worth.

I hope you'll not lose hope, although the West
has wrapped you in its freedom, made you feel
its shapeless weight upon your shoulders pressed.
Asphyxiation is a new ordeal
designed to stifle any old ideal
of reverence for life, or candle-flame
of guttering God within each human frame.

*   *   *

The anchoress of Norwich, Mother Julian,
experienced nothing wrathful in God's nature
but a loving boundlessness, compassion,
like motherhood, of a sustaining nurture,
source and ground of being, in such manner
that none need feel disconsolate, deserted:
We hold each other goodly comforted.

Of him and her, the human condition,
Simone Weil probed the truth, and led
the way, not avoiding grave affliction;
and Heloise outsuffered Abelard:
for women are the battered face of God.
Men have been the Marys, women Marthas
who die unpublished, unacknowledged martyrs.

*   *   *

Unknown to me at first, I must confess
the master-poet, Homer, I have found . . .
though most remote from me in time and place,
like Keats, I am bewildered and spellbound
at last exploring this long-hidden ground.
Can the hand of some momentous fate
have led me thus to Homer, though so late?

As if I was not ready in my youth
to hear the song or learn the singer's art;
as if some ancient or unwelcome truth
is urgent now, would press upon my heart,
that through my efforts it might play a part
in plucking us from hubris-extinction
in making this old world Christ's new creation.

*   *   *

Not one of us but needs a guru now.
Where shall I find the teachers meant for me?
Are they alive? and if I meet them, how
shall I know them? And in what surety
can I submit to their authority?
No sign but the mode of contradiction,
the living body marked by crucifixion.

My present helpers are unknown to me.
Perhaps I spoke with one of them today.
"My greatest teacher is my enemy"
I heard the quiet Tibetan exiles say.
To kick against the goad? More hope that way
than if I feel no hurt within the shell
of my apparent duties performed well.

Know myself! and know with whom I'm dealing:
"I am," said God, who needs no predicate.
Of that great absolute I am revealing
the whole within myself in tiny part
and nothing can detract from that one whit:
"I am" beyond all category or sect.
I, in becoming human, am perfect.

*   *   *

And so I write to you "My dearest him"
unknown to me and yet close to my heart.
"I" and "Thou," sense of seraphim

enlarging me, yet pulling me apart:
refining alchemy, purest art
of transformation—let me now be changed
as our self-substances are rearranged.

And not just you and I as a couple
but others in a noosphere of love;
one teacher is another's disciple. . . .
Who is then the master, who the slave?
What can I give unless I first receive,
and how receive unless I struggle free
to follow the next teacher calling me . . . ?

BETWEEN OURSELVES

Between ourselves and the universe
there is only skin
that exists in perpetual cellular birth and death.

Between ourselves and the universe
there is only the self-renewal of skin
as it interacts with waves,
with revolving particles and immense particulars.

Leaves have veins
birds their wings
and animals their delicate nostrils.

We have only our skins
between us and that which kills
or heals or heals or kills,
sustains or slowly extinguishes—
and skin, living cover of planet Earth.

Skin is alive with mind
and we have mind
between ourselves and the universe;

mentality, our attitudes
our ways of thinking about ourselves
and the Earth among the stars.

We can renew our minds as we do our skins
and think relatedly:
related to the stars,
to one another
and to that separated self
who shares our skin, our planet.

DOWRY

We bring treasure
in a casket, sealed,
gifted by family,
inherited, held,
passed on with honour.
>   We make it our own
>   in thought and fantasy,
>   all that we cherish
>   work for, nourish:
>   the loved and the known.

Believe in treasure
but don't look inside
the box, wanting proof.
Nothing's to hide
in what's beyond measure.
>   Does it seem empty?
>   Is it not enough?
>   We cannot disclose
>   something that grows.
>   Let's share this plenty.

VOICE IN THE NIGHT

If passion slows to tempo of a blues
lament and pain sharpens the shoulder blade
and still my arm goes down to finger tips
and friendly voice is gravelly with death
residing in the throat, so that the song
itself of life is blistered through with note
of its mortality and mine, which might
be sooner than my mother's in her failing
wits, and leave my lover lonely, who
has given me a taste of what it is
to lose, the more to find, my singing soul. . . .

I'll no longer lie in the dark, but rise,
put on the light, consult whatever serves
as oracle, without a pilgrimage
save that of Lao Tsu or Socrates
or Christ and those interpreters of theirs,
who may have heard the crazy voices that
directed them to seek an early death
for an imaginative cause that made
the world too good to leave unsacrificed.

I'll tell my children not to suffer fools
nor think themselves unwise in judging from
experience, and living at the highest
point of contradiction, where
music breaks from human bitterness
and simple gestures of the mind or mood
transcend such limits as engender them.

III

TURN YOURSELF ABOUT

LESS IN THOUGHT THAN IN LOVE

It isn't because I've loved you
for more than seven years
that I made this pilgrimage.

It isn't because your eyes are olive
your hair like coppery earth
your voice like shadow of trees.

It isn't because I missed you
or needed consolation, or
had something I wanted to say.

I knew you were accompanied
by one I rejoiced to see you with,
young, fair, loveable.

I knew myself in the deepening
of my years, the downward spiral,
my sun obscured with tears.

I knew the light I lived by
withdrawn, unless I labour
to kindle it daily myself.

I knew that to seek the sun
or history in its majesty
cannot restore the present.

I made this tedious journey
because to remain at home
would have been renunciation:

not acceptance of destiny
or sacrifice to the gods
or purification of life,

but a forsaking of that
which has to utter "I am,"
which awakes, less in thought than in love.

THE WHITE STONE OF LEWIS

Do not attempt
to lift the white stone.
It is smooth quartzite
and weighs a lifetime.

You would prove your back
could take the strain;
brave, ambitious
you could handle any challenge.

But another strength is more sustaining:
able to change and take changes
lift old habits from heavy soil
get to grips with the stone surface
of self-deception.

Let those do the heaving and shoving
who shoulder burdens they cannot manage
and set their sights on defeating others
in aimless shows of strength.

You carry the stone within you
light with humour
crystal with hope
smooth with complete integrity.

SEAHOOD

On a headland pine trees
stand in their shadows.
Around them the ocean
swirls in a thousand eyes
of light, and sings
its ageless song of worlds
and red rocks,
of diving birds and their wings
flying beneath the waves,
of tiny plants and creatures
that live because of the tide
and its wayward faithfulness.

Unthought-of happinesses
shall occur, shall become of us,
because of the seahood we enter
in each other,
the distant travels, adventures
each of us brings ashore.

MIND'S LOVE

I've loved you with all my heart and soul and strength
but not with my mind.
Such mindless love is not good enough for you.

I loved you with my heart and it only hurt
because the heart is rash and ridiculous.
I loved you with my soul and it became
a tedious recital of unattained perfection.
I loved you with my strength and it left me weak
without supporting you.

To love with the mind is the only way
to love at all.
But how is it done?
By darkness, silence, rain, absence,
a hundred negatives?
By light, space, dancing, walking
over hills or along the beach?
By books, discussion, policy-making?
By lying all night together
without a word or touch
but the presence of the other
filling the lonely world?

To love with the mind
is to piece together a patchwork from all of these,
adapted to the occasion;
to lay aside all plans of happiness,
all friends or enemies,
shapes from the past
or shadows in the present.

It is to penetrate the exactitude
of how you feel and what you mean to say;
and to respond with the appropriate note
of assurance, acceptance
of separate identity
and merged, yet heightened, humanity.

TO EACH LOVE ITS SORROW

Gaelic, they say, they sing, they weep,
has thirteen words for love
and nineteen for sorrow.

Each love brings its own
peculiar, multiple sorrows;
greens and greys
are finely distinguished;
colours flow like sounds
into each other, like lines
in a carved design, like the stream,
like raindrops at the sea's edge
plashing their shiny ripples
and running away on the tide,
like mist at the mountain cliff.

A true Gael is green or
blue-grey of the pale cheek
from grief and waiting.

What colour shall I choose?

My bush-soul has sickened,
my dream-soul has withered,
my ancestral-soul has ceased
to re-incarnate.
And I? What colour am I?

A song out of memory,
or the face of one
who has made a long journey,
or the voice of one who has suffered
and still sings.

Love is expansion,
a waxing of mind and spirit,
but sorrow breathes out,
clenches and contracts,
grips and squeezes to the last drop.

It catches the dream
and pours out its waters
in grey, black, dun, dusky,
brindle, dapple.

Such is the stained sorrow
that blanches the heart like mist
when compassion finds no form.

Love is ceaselessly liquid,
dark its interior,
but none can see the depth
or source
and water drains away
into the greedy earth
or casual, cloudy silence.

Red, chestnut, tawny, noble,
strong, golden, true, bright,
tinctured, pure, delicate:
such are the colours of love
that has outlived its sorrow.

LEAVE IT TO THE DIRKS

If God is in it (and there's no knowing)
leave it between ourselves and the dirks.
— GAELIC SAYING

If god be in it, or it be of god,
(and there's no knowing);
if it be in the destined nature of things
or, like a miracle, bound to happen
once the conditions prevail;
if darkness be in it at once with light,
this with that and long with short;
if it appears on the thresholds of time and place;
if there is no knowing beyond
our knowing we cannot know;
if to understand we would have to surrender
our point of view
or previously-held convictions
or inculcated habits
of thought (looking for proof);
if there's a chance in it of profit
to one of us, and no
apparent harm to the world
or the least of the children;
if opposing is likely to strengthen its arm
and supporting is likely to strengthen ours;
if our aims are clear in our heads
and the means we choose for achieving them
are pure as our hearts and clean
as our hands that daily, properly work for them;

then do not attempt to interfere or regulate
or determine the outcome in any way;
do not destroy by guile or by straight attack;
do not stamp on shoots that are growing
or silence the questions:

"Leave it to the dirks"
when criteria are lacking
by which conclusions can be drawn.

The dirk will come to the point,
cut clean, draw blood,
will make incision, decision,
take sides, divide,
sacrifice the good for the better.
The dirk will prove us,
test our position and claim
our authority as makars of ourselves.
We'll win or lose
kill or surrender
do or die
but we'll not negotiate again
or allow ourselves to be netted with ambiguity,
to be cheated again with smiles
or dispossessed of our land, our language, our memory.

CRY OUT AND SAY

I want you to love me
love me enough
enough that it hurts
hurts and you cry
cry out and say
say you love me.

Love me today
today and tomorrow
tomorrow when older
older yet fonder
fonder means deeper
deeper in love.

I want you to open
open your arms
arms that defend
defend your feelings
feelings you hide
hide your sorrow.

I want you to laugh
laugh at defeat
defeat despair
despair no more
more means ever
ever and after.

TRANSFORMATION

Inch by inch we are rolling the stone away,
the boulder wedged across our light.
If we relent for an instant
we lose more than we gained
in the previous heave.

No angel performs the task while we sleep.
No one remembers how it came
about that we were buried
taken for dead and dankly
left in the cave.

Stifled by fear that others may cease to help
each one leaving it to the rest,
we, in perpetual dark,
suspect we are only exhausting
ourselves for nothing.

Is there a secret crevice in the stone,
a cleavage where the lines of weakness
cross and coalesce,
that blunted, groping fingers
might discover?

Or, through our utmost effort and energy,
our calculations, trials and errors,
our loss of hope and moments
of apathy, do we ourselves expand
and crack the shell?

MODERATION

This moderate love drives me to extremes.
Pythagorean proportion makes for shape,
harmonious sound and visual satisfaction.
How can I construct my daily life
in ratio? Keep rounded humours squared?
Let none exceed its own appointed limits?

I cannot find such rule within to measure,
to modify, prevent my swings and falls.
Religion never proffers middle ground:
Christ with his "leave all and follow me";
Buddha's wise: "let go, detach, walk on";
Islam's submissiveness and arrogance.
They ultimately claim and contradict,
tell us to work out our own salvation.

The algebra we need for this is not
in any book, and when we get it wrong
we can't go back and do the sum again.
But complications crowd onto the page
until we know that nothing equals X
or X is more than equal everything.
What we believe or long for is unproved
except by pain, which is love's formula.

I'll look for balance and the golden mean,
but such restraint itself may generate
its own unproven postulates; and seek
a sum, the square on some hypotenuse
equal to the forms, polygonal,
immoderate, unpredictable, of love.

single

dark loch and single swan
sails alone

flock of twenty wintered here
familiar

one was killed and flopped dead
in its blood

the mate remains isolated
neck twisted

always as if expecting
sudden wing

dips the serpent head below
in deeper woe

this lonely silent bright one
with its reflection

MOVING HOME

I leave you, nest,
we twig by twig constructed,
lined with our feathers,
warmed with our devotion,

centre of celebration,
babies, poems, reunions, friendship,
night-long confidings,
tears, rage, peace.

I know the story of this carpet stain,
that broken chair,
why the flex did not stretch,
where sunlight reaches in this season.

I know the Braid Hills contour
before a winter moon
pacing by the window
soothing babies.

In this kitchen I can work by touch.
The bathroom is aware of my dimensions.
The garden, too, I know its underground.

Goodbye lilac tree!
What do you mean to me
but a decadent kind of purity?

Goodbye fuchsia, buddleia,
roses, daffodils, blaze of broom.
You should be safe in your earth beds
from our human upheavals.

Goodbye table
where I've typed all night
then crept to bed at early light
too tired to sleep
mentally roused.

Goodbye my golden bedroom.

Clinging to the house are patches of each child:
they shall haunt me no longer.
They have left their childish skins
grown and flown in lustre and in dreams.

I leave, I go, walk ahead
toward simplicity.
No new nest
secure branch,
but a precipice
receiving views, wilder shores,
a landing ledge and launching stage
for new migrations
exquisite, far imaginings.

MEDITATION AFTER SEPARATION

My decision to leave
I do not regret
nor my decision to join him
silver years ago.

We must make believe:
we must make up our minds
and our minds compose us.

I miss him and it hurts.
I weep thoughtdrops
for habitual tenderness,
unstinted husbandry.

There are some who disapprove
of any sign of weakness
or self-deprecation
so I refrain
from formulating feelings.

*   *   *

Mary was contrary,
opposites combined in her without conflicting:
silver bells and cockle shells,
pretty maids lined up
as they stand in Greenham Common
ringed around the brutal fence
absorbing contradictions:
weapons for peace?
humans cause for danger?

In recesses of the will
primed with intention
focused on each other
we possess as it is
the most sure weapons
with which to hurt each other:

and each of us is hurt
according to capacity.

I wanted not to be hurt again
but when we love
we structure ourselves for compassion,
no longer distinguish friend from enemy.

Was not my mind made up
over educated aeons
by men and their principles
like leaden bars across my stained glass?

Little things are important
        but not my little worries. . . .
He is important
        but I am not to fuss. . . .
I was a bad example as a mother:
suddenly, after twenty years
of singing in the cage,
I wept in front of the children.

He put a cloth over me.

My mind is made up by much contrariness
and when I see him hurt
I want to take him in my arms,
but to touch him now is not allowed
when once it was commanded.

I admit I miss him unspeakably
and so I do not mention it.

I perch on a ledge.
It's no place for laying eggs
or feathering with poems.

That was in the old nest.

Now I learn to fly
but cannot sing at the same time.

The singing was within the cage
the flying silent.

DREAMS

We enter each other's dreams
by way of the flesh.
It may take years of unsevered love
before we dream of each other.

In dreams there is no divorce.
In mine you are always taking part
and it's never any surprise.
You are young in my dreams,
young, and you simply belong.

No one can take my place
in dreaming of you.

IN PRAISE OF
'C.K.'

Calm, old, gentle, gracious
the strength of your youth
and its beauty have concentrated
themselves into elegance.

The forces that formed you
and drove you to achieve
with certainty and precision
the excellence you expected

of yourself, of others,
are gathered now and
shine like polished wood
or underwater pebbles.

I cherish the dignity
you manifest, this sense
that life can be in order
and the order bountiful.

IN PRAISE OF
THE WORLD, THE FLESH AND THE DEVIL

Order of the snake: on the silver chalice
Twines a tree as handle, with climbing serpent.
This my christening present, my Indian birthright,
Sacred religion.

World our home, our habitat, where we shelter;
World we love as mother and father, giving
Breath and substance, all that sustains the human.
Earth is our Heaven.

Flesh the seamless garment that clothes our person
Binds us, pairs us, keeps our identity and
Makes a holy trinity through relations:
Born of each other.

Jesus teaches love of our enemy and
Love of neighbour equal to love of self, but
Self includes the shadow within; poor devil
Needs our acceptance.

Fruit and river, god of the olive garden;
Nothing can destroy our redemptive working
Close to earth, yet spiralling upward; serpent,
Sign of our wisdom.

THE WATER-CARRIERS

A water-carrier, meeting another, asked him for some of his water.
The latter said, "Why don't you drink your own?" The first said,
"Give me some of your water, for I am sick of my own."
— from *The Conference of the Birds* (FARID UD-DIN ATTAR)

A drop, a pearl
from your cup poured
better than fountain,
rain or cloud;

      as my soul,
      disquieted,
      seeks to drink,
      so pure it flows
      through all, to sink
      or rise again,
      but never rests,
      save in the valley
      of emptiness.

Heavy the weight
our own life fills.
I offer my cup—
it brims and spills
your thirst to slake:

      we give, we take.

RICHES

They come with gold sewn into their clothes
sewn in for those who have none.
    —from *The Drunkards* by Rumi, trs Robert Bly

They have gold sewn into their clothes,
pouches hidden beneath
their beggarly garments.

You cannot tell from their faces
or hands or the way they walk
that they are rich.

Nothing from them is expected.
They impart to others
what was not consciously asked.

From them we each receive
the gold. It is our own worth—
beyond possessions.

PEN FRIENDS

*Inspired by letters between Pasternak,
Rilke and Tsvetaeva, 1926*

To write letters
love letters
to real people
line after line of imaginary love,
untouched by detail
age, habit, gender,
by distance, attachments,
by even the body itself,
its distracting beauty
or gradual deterioration:

I'll write to *you*, then, and *you:*
you, whom I've never met
except in your letter-making;
you, whom I've met
but hardly know
not seen your home
watched you eat, sleep;
you, who wrote to me
and began a story that
caught us in its dictation
again and again
because we believed it,
found our lives, without that image, false.

Do not regret such letters
self that I became;
or castigate
the person within who wrote them.
Reality is beyond our bounds,
our caution, our second thought.

By casting it in letters
we set love free.

SLEEPLESSNESS

My head pulses to the moaning of the wind
and I am at the mercy of my mind
which takes me back and forth across
this storm of life and all my night.

Night is time whose point is made in death
and every growth a threshold crossed with no return
to make amends or give
a different emphasis or cadance to
the hard-wrought poem it is
to live at all in love.

From whom I have received I have been formed
and dreamed alive;
in turn have given others what I hardly knew
I was.

To strive for reciprocity is vain and leads
to jangled insufficiencies.
We neglect the shine of life in us
if, clogged with over-faithfulness,
we fail to let it lighten whom it may.
Dimitte nobis debita nostra.

Forgive our trespassing where
we do not belong,
though we may not discover this
until we've wandered far and
settled deep,
as others do in us and leave
their trampled track
gates open,
but fruits also,
seeds of future flowers.

The night is not for sleep
but for journeys of the mind and memory.

87

REDEDICATION

Geese are threading their skein
with clamour
between the stars of Orion
as he strides the river of sky
upholding the moon on high
who casts her dominion
into my room, my head
and sets alight my nerves
so that awake I cry
and fly in thought
around and between the world
and its peoples
poisoned like weeds in India
the peasants, the poor in their hovels
starving in Ethiopia
exposed on their man-made desert
and our television screens.

My own afflictions
cannot be cured by moonlight
but by each day rising
however serious the night
and its dreams, asleep or awake,
however tinged with aching the dawn;
by rising
to pit my powers with those
who will to create
and clamour against the destroyers
wasters of substance;
by rising up with anger
against their slumbering blunders
their fears, discourtesies,
but leading them to lend
their weight, their belts, their boots
to work of salvation
one by one
for us all.

BLACK GOLD

Black miners sweat for gold
White powers manufacture weapons
Economics rules the world.

Weapons serve economics
Gold gives power to the whites
Whose world depends on black miners.

Weapons turned on black miners
Power of white economics
The world is worth its weight in gold.

Gold is sheer economics
Weapons do not feed the world
Black power undermines the whites.

Economical black miners
Gold is turned into weapons
White power destroys the world.

ICONS

The greatest feast of all:
Christ in *the Mandorla*
gold, before the ruined gates of Hell,
stretches out a hand to
Adam and Eve released
by this, his rise, his Resurrection.

Icon resurrected
stripped to original
revealed, restored by removing layers
to cinnabar, ochre
pearls on robes of heroes
under blackened paint of centuries.

HORSES

Florus and Laurus, saints
of herdsmen, finders of
strayed horses; from left to right see how
they gallop! The angel
rides fiery-winged, raised hands
joined by a rainbow. Eyes stare up, now

knocked into a horse-trough,
crates for potatoes, boards
for gaping windows, hacked, burnt, thrown on
the scrap-heap; whence an old
secret woman scrapes them:
hers the entreaty, theirs the suff'ring.

90

RESCUE

Rescued the feeble
cloistered in a kitchen
saved what could save: cruelly beautiful
Virgin of tenderness
who heals, who salves, healing
needs, with him who leans against her cheek.

The Saviour's cheek, his brow
on Veronica's veil,
his face, his eyes, *not made with hands*, but
fallen into our hands;
fallen, himself the WAY;
the Saviour saved, plucked from the burning.

Emmanuel—he is
no longer in church or
holy place, but in our safe-keeping:
Child, enthroned no longer
save in our blue and gold
or pearled life of an ancient woman.

PROTECTOR AND PROPHET

Intercessor, bishop,
St Nicholas, and blesser
of Russian folk in town or village.
His sword could not protect
city or holy place,
destroyed lest still they work their powers.

In flame Elijah, as
Apollo charioted,
throws down his fur cape to Elisha
who takes upon himself
the prophet's fate: and now?
An old sick man keeps the disused key.

TRUTH

Broken church, stabbed dragon,
slaughtered again they do
not die. Layer by layer we simplify,
seek our own origin,
experience desctruction—
for truth, an image we rely on.

MARTYRS

Dimness of the past is
too bright for the present:
faded, they draw us yet toward grace.
Put to a thousand deaths
the icons are martyred
elements dismembered, without trial.

They should go by water
floated down the decades
holy image facing sun and trees;
woodwork and minerals,
gesso and artistry
returned to the source whence they derived.

ELEMENTS

Enthroned, *Pantocratur*
Christ within the cosmos
infinitely blue, shows the gospel:
"Come unto me all ye,
ye workers and peasants,
whose collective labour built churches

and now has struck them down."
We shall all return to
Sofia in whom elements consist.
Saints and martyrs, leaders
of soviets, protest!
These images, their word, may not fail.

92

THE TOWER

(An allegory)

On a path beside the cliffs
midst camomile and rosemary
olives and yellow broom
among *papillons* and sudden wings:
les petits oiseaux d'or
I was summoned to the ascent.

I turned my back on the shore
where sunlit ocean repeatedly
strafes the coast in fountains of whitest foam
and I began the climb.

My guide planted his feet where stones held firm.
He trod down briers
and parted tangled branches.
I fixed my eyes on the ground
to note where his step had marked
the crumbling scree,
to watch where his fingers grasped
the knife-edged rocks.
He did not turn and I followed in silence.
Where the rock-face was sheer
and overhanging the narrow track
I managed on my own
knowing his hand was near.

Up and around, round and upward
through thicket and over stony ledge
I asked "Have we reached halfway?"
"Halfway" was his reply
and every time I questioned . . .
until I raised my head and saw the tower.

The path was wider now, more open to the sun
but pine-trees offered shade.
Despite thirst and pain
I was glad to know the end in sight—
and shining by the wayside
was the purple peony.

I rested to survey
mountain behind mountain
with the encircling sea,
tortuous routes, homes,
the dwelling-places of my life
its journeys plotted out,
all far below and *diminished*
for I had passed beyond them.

We stumbled on toward the tower
and stopped beside it.
"It is high enough" I said.
"You must climb the tower"—
my guide was smiling.

Rungs of iron were soldered
into the perpendicular walls.
I gazed up, afraid,
for my knees were weak with climbing
and my hands in ribbons
from laceration of rock and twig.

I saw the ladder led into upper darkness.
"I cannot climb the tower."
But my guide was wise and merciless:
"You will do it."

In weakness I closed my hands on the iron rails
placed my feet on the lowest bar
and step by step, reach by reach,
dragged my body upwards
until I bowed my head to crawl into
the cavern of the tower.
It was completely dark.

But it was not the end:
again I had to strive,
round up my scattered courage,
grope for another ladder.

In darkness now I mounted,
struggled up and round until
I crept onto the very roof,
the summit of the tower.
Legs, arms, hands, even my lips and face
were trembling with fatigue:

It was accomplished.

MY INDIAN SELF

Let me be
myself my
Indian self
that goes to extremes
from garland to ashes
Himalaya to desert
mango to maize.

Let me wear the silks,
the sandals and the gold.
Let me dip my fingers
in the bowl of desire
even here in the puritan
corners of my dwelling.

Let me reclaim
myself. I cannot
be curtailed.
Extravagance is my form
not my style.
Intensity is how
my pulse is rated.

My body is myself
however ageing.
I love the way it has borne
with me all these years
and given nothing less
than life itself to others.

Happiness is tropical and
love is a house with wide verandahs.
Joy is my element.
I pass it through the test
of water, fire, air
and bring it back to earth.